All About a Boy Who Was Afraid of Thunder

(And How He Got Over It)

Ann Marie Hannon
A "Kids With Worries" Book®

Paperback: 978-1-63767-168-9
eBook: 978-1-63767-169-6
Library of Congress Control Number: 2021918300

Grade K-4
Literary Fiction
A "Kids with Worries" Book®
The Second Story in the Grandma Annie Chronicles

Ordering Information:

BookTrail Agency
8838 Sleepy Hollow Rd.
Kansas City, MO 64114

Printed in the United States of America

TABLE OF CONTENTS

Chapter 1
At Grandma's House

oday, there's a sky overhead filled with huge puffy dark clouds that are streaming across the horizon. Those clouds seem angry and mean to me. They only allow split second flickers of light to shine through bits of open sky.

That threatening sky reminds me of when I was a kid and afraid of thunder. I would see clouds like those moving closer and closer and I'd become very worried and afraid. I knew a warm, pleasant summer day might change to heavy, pelting rain with bolts of lightning and horrible crashing thunder.

I also knew that would make me put my hands over my ears and run and hide. Even if I was safe in my house, I would still cover my ears and run and hide under my bedcovers.

I was lucky, though. I would have gone on worrying and being afraid of thunder if it hadn't been for a lovely lady who helped me and still helps youngsters solve normal, everyday, but critical for a kid, worries.

Are you curious to find out more? Okay, then let's go.

Somewhere on a little hill overlooking a tiny town there is a house where that lovely lady lives. Her name is Grandma Annie. I've just driven up the little hill because I'm visiting Grandma Annie, just to say hello, and to ask her if there is anything she needs. I won't stay long, because she's already told me that she must visit one of her grandchildren this evening to help him with a worry about thunder.

You know what a worry is I'm sure.

Understandably all kids and even grownups have worries from time to time and Grandma Annie is glad to help anyone with a worry including her grandchildren.

Right now, as I mentioned, I'm stopping by just to say hello and to see if there is anything that she needs. Most of the time, when that happens she asks me back, "Is there anything that you need, honey?"

It makes me chuckle when that happens. Thanks to Grandma Annie, I am always respectful and polite to say, "I already have everything I need, Grandma, because you were there for me a long time ago."

I always love visiting Grandma Annie and I stop by to say, hello, as often as I can. Let's just knock on her front door, and see how she's doing. She has a new security camera device so she can see who is there. I like to knock three times, then ring the doorbell so she knows it's me even though she can of course see me in the camera. It's our secret knock.

"Hello Grandma. How are you doing today?"

"Hello, and welcome," says a voice from behind the door.

I know that a small wisp of a lady with abundant silvery hair, wearing a pretty frock and walking using a small cane is answering the doorbell ring and my secret knock.

"Oh Grandma, it's only me, and I'm waiting out here and it's really cold, and cloudy, brrr."

"Hello, Brendan," she calls through the security microphone. "Please come in. I've just unlocked the door. Come in come in, always so happy to see you."

"Hi Grandma, I'm just as happy to see you and I won't stay long. I know you're going to visit Grandson Number 5," I say, laughing out loud.

"Oh Brendan, you always like to joke," but Grandma even chuckles herself about calling all of her grandchildren by numbers.

Still talking, we walk carefully down the hallway toward the living room.

"Yes, Jimmy had a worrisome experience recently and now because of that he has a worry that I'm going to help him solve."

"Hah, if anyone can help it's you."

"His mom and dad can always help, but there is a lot happening with planning for the new brother or sister; so I've been asked to help."

"I'm sure you can help; you always helped me when I was younger. You still help me too, because you make me happy when I can just visit here and speak with you."

"Why thank you, Brendan, that's an honor coming from you. All children have worries from time to time."

We reach the living room and Grandma Annie sits down. She smiles, "So, can you tell me what's going on and why I have the pleasure of you visiting today?"

"Well, I just wanted to say hello and ask if you needed anything," I say, politely, smiling to myself, "And I know you are going to say you are fine."

"There's another reason why I'm here too. I want to introduce you to some friends of mine who heard about you and want to meet you."

"Oh my, that's interesting. I don't see them though."

"Well, they are reading all about you in my latest book. Remember I was always worried that I couldn't write and that my teachers thought I would be better off working as an engineer or a doctor?"

"Yes, I remember." Grandma added, "It made me sad, but you didn't give up."

"Well, my first book won an award and I'm now working on my next book and I want my readers to meet you in the story and to learn from you all about how to overcome worries."

"Well, that's a tall order, honey. Do you think I can do that?"

"I know you can! To help, I've brought you a small tape recorder so you can record any of the stories you want to share about worries and how to get over them. Just start whenever you have time.

"Hmm, I like that idea. It's sort of lonely here from time to time and I miss having lots of children here. But, if I can tell my stories in this way, that will make me use my imagination in a way that will make me feel happy by helping someone with the stories I tell."

"Yes, Grandma. It's all set." I chuckle, delightedly." Here's the button to start and once you start just get comfortable and talk in the same way that you like to talk to your own grandchildren, including me. Let's see how it goes now, before you have to leave to visit Jimmy."

"Okay," Grandma smiles and holds the recorder lightly in her hand.

"Great," I say with a sigh of relief. "Use your imagination to say hello to all the readers who want to hear your stories."

I sit down and take a moment to absorb being here too.

I have always loved Grandma Annie's house. It's small, but filled with lots of natural light. In the living room on winter evenings and even during early spring and late fall, there is always a gently burning fire log in the living room fireplace. On the piano in the living room there are loads of family pictures. And the entire room is painted in what Grandma calls, robin eggshell blue. This softens the light in a remarkable way, but Grandma's rocking chair and the small table next to it are the most important items and that's where she sits when telling all the stories that help to solve many normal fears and worries.

Grandma places the recorder on the little table next to her rocker. Starting to rock, slowly, she begins, "Hello and welcome. I think I've met you before. I'm Grandma Annie. Have you come to hear another story about kids with worries? I hope so. I'm always happy to share my stories because all children have worries from time to time. My stories help to solve those worries in new and useful ways. So, today's story is all about being afraid of thunder and how to get over it. I'm going to tell this story to my grandson. His picture is right there on the piano and he's holding his Teddy Bear, named Theodore. I just found out that he is afraid of thunder. He told me on the phone about a terrible thunderstorm that happened recently that made him very afraid. So, I'm going to visit him, and I think I can help. I'm going to tell him a story that his Grandpa told me about when Grandpa was a boy and he was afraid of thunder. I'm on my way now for a visit. You come too."

"That's great, Grandma, just click the button again and it will close. Thanks, so much. I can just imagine what's happening at Jimmy's house while he's waiting for you to arrive."

"Hah, ha. I agree. Jimmy loves his Teddy Bear and they are always together. I'm sure that he's speaking with his "Teddy" right now, and his "Teddy" is talking back to him. You see, I know that Jimmy needs a friend and up until the new brother or sister arrives, he's the only child in the house. So, I think Jimmy uses his imagination to speak with his "Teddy" and that's okay because using imagination is exercise for the brain just like riding a bicycle is exercise for the arms and legs."

"You do have a way of explaining things, Grandma." I compliment her again. "I'll be on my way now so you can get going. I had a wonderful visit; can't wait for your story."

"Oh, I will get it to you honey. Just sitting and using my imagination to make the recording so far was enjoyable. I felt like there were loads of wonderful children listening. I'll make sure I finish it, but for now, I'd better get going too. Love you."

I helped Grandma to her car and noticed the earlier threatening sky had moved on. The setting sun was shining, and it gave me peace to know at least for today Jimmy would not have to endure another frightening thunderstorm.

Seeing a bright late-day sky also made me feel sure about "Grandma Annie to the rescue" and that she would help Jimmy. I saw her again much later and the results I learned about her visit were amazing.

Chapter 2
At Jimmy's House

"**H**ere we go again!", said Theodore, as he jumped up and down on Jimmy's bed. It's about thunder. Right?"

You have just met Theodore, Jimmy's "teddy". Yes, I'm still here to help explain that Grandma is on her way to visit Jimmy and I've left for my own home, But because I know so much about Grandson Number 5, I am pretty sure what I tell you here is very close to what occurred.

"So glad you got over your "afraid of the dark" worries, Jimmy-boy." Theodore always likes to joke with Jimmy, "I never had a clue about your next worry."

Jimmy smiles back at Theodore, "Well, it happens to the best of us, Theodore!"

"I know why you have that new worry too," Theodore says casually. "Remember a few weeks ago, how you were totally scared during the storm because of the terribly loud thunder and flashes of lightning. You clutched on to me so tightly I thought my teddy bear stuffing was going to pop. Then you tried hiding under the bed, only after you were hiding under the bed covers, and finally you hid both of us in your closet. Both of us!"

"I know, I know," giggles Jimmy." It was so funny, but I'm still sort of worried about the next time we get another storm and if there's thunder like that one."

"Well, Jimmy," chortles Theodore, "I'm glad that Grandma Annie is coming here before anything like that happens again. She helped you when you were "afraid of the dark". I'm sure she will know exactly how to help you now."

"Well, Mom said that Grandma Annie had a story to tell me that would help. I hope she will help you too, since you were just as worried and afraid, as I was."

"But she doesn't know that you talk to me and I talk to you. Right?"

"I know. But, if she did know, it's okay, because she would say that it's a good thing and I'm using my imagination."

"Well, I don't care what you call it; I'm here for you buddy. Whenever you're afraid, I'm afraid. Whenever you have worries, I have worries. You can count me in!" chimes Theodore. "Hey, how about a high-5 handshake?"

They both laughed, and did not hear the knock on the door, or see Grandma Annie entering. She had left her cane in the car and told them she was "furniture-surfing." That made them giggle. She promised to be careful though.

"Hello, I missed visiting you so much! How are you doing? I remember on the phone you told me you were afraid of thunder and worried about a thunderstorm happening again!"

"Oh! Hello, Grandma! Yes, I'm really worried about that. Will you help me," holding his teddy bear closely, "and Theodore?"

"Why, of course, isn't that what grandmas are for? So, Mom and Dad can handle other important things and grandmas can help their grandchildren with stories that solve their worries," says Grandma Annie, smiling.

"Now I hope you are not too surprised when I tell you thunder is a good thing. Yes, it's very good and there is an important reason why. Turns out that thunder helps you to know when it's time to stay inside and sheltered, so the dangerous lightning doesn't harm you."

Jimmy does look surprised, "How can thunder be a good thing when it scares me so much and makes me so worried? Are you sure?"

Grandma is happy to answer, "That's because thunder is like a lot of other noises that are also good, and loud like thunder, but that can still make you worried unless you solve it. It's important to think about that. Would you be surprised to know thunder is a good thing like the loud strong whistleblowing that happens to start a race? "

Jimmy seemed still a bit confused, and then looked quickly at Theodore. I'm almost sure that Jimmy's imagination was working, and Theodore spoke back. If so, it would likely have been something like, "She's got a point there. Those racing whistles are loud!"

Theodore always had a way with words so I'm sure Jimmy smiled then and waited for Grandma Annie to continue.

"How about someone knocking loudly on your front door to let you know there may be danger in the area, and you need to stay indoors," questioned Grandma.

"See," Theodore was whispering unbeknownst to Grandma, "I remember when there was a stray racoon roaming around the neighborhood and the Vet services guy knocked on everyone's door to let them know it wasn't safe to be outside until they caught the racoon because it may have had rabis that awful disease that can hurt humans."

"That makes sense, Grandma," Jimmy agrees, "What else?"

Grandma Annie responds, "There are many other loud sounds that may scare us at first but are good things to have because they keep us safe. Even if thunder is very loud, it is also good because if we didn't have thunder it sure would be hard to know about staying out of the way of dangerous lightning."

Grandma Annie sits down and says, "But I agree that thunder is also a challenge because of its sound! It is loud and even scary; you can choose to meet the challenge though by being focused and counting like I'm going to teach you. Did you know that thunder can help you to know how far away that lightning is?"

"Really, Grandma?" Jimmy questions, "How can that be?"

"Well, I'll tell you how, if you jump under the covers into bed and get ready to go to sleep."

"Okay, Grandma!" Jimmy made a quick jump onto his bed holding Theodore as he jumped. "How's that for a jump?"

Grandma Annie giggles, "Okay very good, but not too much jumping. We don't want to ruin the mattress."

Later I learned Grandma then moved and sat down on the rocker reserved for her in Jimmy's room and she placed the recorder I'd given her on the table nearby. She had found that making the recordings was so interesting she had brought the recorder with her that evening. Jimmy and Theodore giggled when they noticed, so Grandma told them what she was doing and then taught them something new and exciting that Jimmy will always remember.

She said, "Before I explain the way to tell how far off the lightening is, I must tell you a story about some children who were all, every single one of them, afraid of thunder and what happened to them during a thunder and lightning storm as a result! It's a story your Grandpa told me about how he learned not to be afraid of thunder when he was just about your age."

Jimmy shuffled around a bit, and then said, "I want to hear the story, but I have something to ask."

"Okay," replied Grandma Annie, "One question before I start. Please, go ahead."

"Well, when you tell the story, is it okay if I want Grandpa, to look like me? Or someone else in the story to look like a friend I have and others to look like other people I know?"

"Why of course. Absolutely. That means you are using your imagination in a wonderful way. Using your imagination is when you let the ideas and pictures of people and places in the story form in your mind. Also, listening to the radio or an audio story is another way to use your imagination. I'm glad you asked. Now, let's see. Where was I?"

"I think you were going to start at, once upon a time, but not too long ago."

"That's right. Okay. So now, just tuck the covers under your chin, and take a deep breath, and let me tell you all about once upon a time, but not too long ago."

Grandma didn't hear, but Theodore, looked at Jimmy and said, "This better be good."

Jimmy didn't mind Theodore's silly remark, and replied, "It will be .... I'm sure."

"Did you say something, honey?" Grandma looked keenly at Jimmy.

"No, Grandma, it's nothing."

If I know Grandma Annie, that's when she simply said to herself, "I think Jimmy talks to Theodore. Anyway, if he does talk to his teddy bear, I'm glad because it shows he is also using his imagination."

Grandma Annie believes in imagination as long as it's used correctly so, I know that the next thing she said was, "Okay, let's get on with our story." I'm sure that right then, she clicked the recorder button too.

Chapter 3
On the School Athletic Field Day Many Years Ago

'll let you hear from Grandma Annie but when she first told it to me, it all started on the day of the annual Middletown Elementary Field Day events which always occurred on the last day of the school year.

The entire class that Grandpa was in had assembled at the school along with all the other classes. There were lots of school buses all lined up to take the kids to the event. When Grandpa was a boy he walked to school and there were no daily buses for students, but the athletic field day was an all-day event and teachers and students and parents who volunteered to help were there to ride to the park grounds. All the children had gathered to take pictures of their class before the trip to Pleasant Valley Park where the field day events were to happen. Grandpa told Grandma Annie that he overheard one classmate named Suzy, talking to another classmate, named Billy and it went something like this.

"Billy are you ready for me to beat you in the 3-legged race?" asked Suzy.

"Hah, Suzy! You'll never beat me. I'm the 3-legged king." boasted Billy.

"But you must have a partner for the 3-legged race, Silly. What if Lenny is your partner too?"

Billy was unimpressed by Suzy's quip; in a very bravado voice, Bill replied, "Don't worry. Lenny is slow but I have a trick or two that would speed him up...that is, if he's my partner."

Suzy wasn't put down by his retort; she asked, "Then, what about the relay race?"

Billy wasn't hampered by that question from Suzy either, "Don't worry; I'll pick the best team!"

Suzy pushed on, "But what if you aren't the team leader?"

"Don't worry," said Billy and standing with legs apart and arms folded, "I have another idea about that, so go on with more ideas and problems, I'll bet that I can still win."

"Oh," Suzy exclaimed, exasperated, "you're such a bragger! But, that's okay. I have a few ideas about winning too. It never hurts to be prepared especially on the last day of the school year!"

Then, jumping up and down, they both yelled, "Yay!!"

"Come on, Suzy, let's get our pictures taken before our school bus leaves for the park."

Once the class pictures were all taken, students climbed on to their respective school buses, and the buses started leaving in one long line. It took about an hour for the buses to reach the outskirts of the town and then arrive at the park area within the huge campground. Everyone had already been told the itinerary for the day including which events were for which grades, given safety instructions for the events and where to find restroom facilities, when and where lunch would be served, and who to go to in case there was an "owie" or a scraped knee or other injury.

So now I'm sure you can picture Grandma Annie telling the story to Jimmy and Theodore. I have to laugh to myself about Theodore but it's okay. Grandma would say Jimmy is just using his imagination and that's a good thing.

Grandma Annie continued her story, and Jimmy listened intently. She almost had an inkling that Theodore looked like he was listening too, as Jimmy held Theodore under his arm.

"So, what does that have to do with being afraid, Grandma? It sounds like that would have been a fun and exciting day. What were the competition events they played? Did Grandpa win, did Suzy or Billy win?"

Grandma Annie answered, "Oh yes, there were many happy and fun events starting with the 3-legged race which Grandpa won, not Billy," she smiled to herself. "It turns out Grandpa's partner was Lenny."

Jimmy persisted, "Did they have a relay race, and softball, and volleyball, and tug of war, and hula hoop?"

"Well, Jimmy," Grandma Annie was quizzical, "I don't believe they had hula hoops when Grandpa was a boy, but yes, I'm sure there was tug of war and a relay race and softball and volleyball. But here is what happened next, and it is all about being afraid and making the wrong choices."

"Ohhhh, what happened?", Jimmy snuggled further on his bed, and listened closely.

"Well, you remember I explained it was a perfectly lovely day. "

Jimmy nodded, and Grandma Annie was surprised that she thought Theodore was nodding too, although it may have been Jimmy just shifting his arm around Theodore.

"Yes, it was, a gorgeous and perfect day, a super fun morning with loads of activities and lunch time didn't come any too soon and all of the children were famished after playing and competing in the morning events of the day. So, at lunch time all the kids were sitting on the ground with their fun lunch box meals having sandwiches with carrot and celery sticks and then ice cream popsicles for dessert. But the day didn't stay perfect after they had all finished their ice cream. Without their realizing it, the sky above the kids had suddenly started getting darker and darker. The afternoon sun was soon gone as the clouds blocked it and those clouds were blowing in and billowing and looking darker and darker so that it almost seemed like evening instead of early afternoon."

"Then what happened?" Jimmy asked quickly.

Grandma responded, and I can tell you from memory exactly what happened. From my recall when I was younger, after lunchtime ended with the delicious ice cream for dessert, and just before the start of the afternoon activities, when the sky became darker and darker and amazing clouds blocked the sunlight, it started to rain. At first, it was just a light sprinkling, but then a stronger sprinkling and then the sprinkling turned to sprinkling heavily and worst of all before anyone knew it, there was a bright streak of lightning and a huge clap of thunder. When that happened, everyone started running in all directions. Now, back to Grandma Annie.

"Suzy and Billy and a few other classmates including Grandpa ran to the foot of a huge tree, they held hands and sat down at the base of the tree. There was a terrible clap of thunder and a very large tree branch fell right to the side of where they were sitting under the tree."

"OMG," said Jimmy to Theodore.

"What, Jimmy?", Grandma turned to look more closely at Jimmy.

"Oh, nothing, I just said OMG, that's, Oh my gosh!"

"Well Jimmy I'm glad you said that because it shows you realize how terrible it was and how dangerous it was for the children, including Grandpa. But what happened next was very critical. The children's teacher had run to where their school bus was parked nearby and most of the class had followed her to their bus, but unfortunately not Billy and Suzy and the remaining classmates including Grandpa. Under the tree had seemed safe until the huge branch had come crashing down so close to them all, and now they were petrified and terrified and too scared to move."

Grandma Annie continued, "It was now up to Ms. Teacher to come to the rescue and save the children from under the tree."

Here is what happened next.

Chapter 4
On the School Bus

"Quick children," yelled Ms. Teacher from the bus to the children under the tree," thunder won't hurt you but lightning will. Under that tree is dangerous, but outside in the open is even more dangerous. So, wait for me to tell you when to run to our school bus. It will be right after the next lightning flash. Start counting when you run , and the thunder won't distract you. Can you hear me? Do you understand what I'm telling you to do?"

"Yes, Ms. Teacher," yelled all the children, including Billy, Suzy, and Grandpa.

I learned later her last name really was Teacher. The children loved calling her Ms. Teacher too.

"We won't move until you tell us first and then we start counting and we run. We pinky promise."

Just as Ms. Teacher had explained, there was another huge clap of thunder that made everyone shudder, including Ms. Teacher. Then, Ms. Teacher said, "I'm going to start to count after the next lightning flash. That's when you start to run.

She took a deep breath, then repeated, " You need to count with me when you run so you won't be distracted by any thunder."

Ms. Teacher waited until there was a streak of lightning, then she started counting loudly enough for the children under the tree to start counting and to run without being afraid of the thunder.

As soon as the next lightning bolt hit, Ms. Teacher started counting loudly, "One and two and three and four..." and quickly also called, "Run, run, run!" as the thunder roared.

Within a few more seconds, the children who had been under the tree were safely on their school bus. "Thank goodness," sighed Ms. Teacher, "You made it!"

As I recall my Grandma telling me this story, several of the children from under the tree were shaking and crying. Ms. Teacher placed a towel around each child's shoulders before helping them to sit down in their school bus seats.

They were all there now on the school bus and safe even though it was still raining terribly with thunder and lightning. Then, Ms. Teacher told them she was very, very sorry. The kids looked quizzically at each other wondering why Ms. Teacher would be sorry.

Ms. Teacher went on to say that she had checked the weather report right up to the time the school buses were going to leave for the field day event. The weather person she spoke with assured her that it looked like it was going to be an awesome day for the event. Ms. Teacher was relieved by this news, then she told the class why she was so sorry.

She was calm but controlled when she spoke, "Even though the weather report was good, I'm very sorry that I didn't give you instructions on what to do in the event of a storm because the weather report was for fair and mild weather and I got busy with all the other goings on in preparation for our trip. We were loading game balls and sacks for the 3-legged race and explaining things to the volunteer parents in addition to taking photos and boarding everyone on the buses and then checking that everyone was accounted for."

Ms. Teacher continued, but halted, when she said, "Today was an awakening for us all on what can happen on a perfectly lovely day. You saw the rain start with no warning. Nobody knew it was coming. Not even the weather reporter, and after the rain started everyone started running everywhere. You may have worried about getting drenched by the rain and so you decided to stay under the huge tree to avoid the rain and not get drenched any more than you were already."

She continued, "But then there was more lightning and a huge clap of thunder. I saw some of your putting your hands over your ears and I saw a streak of lightning in the sky and a huge tree branch fell right near where you were all sitting under the tree."

Grandma's story when she told it to me gave both Suzy and Billy a lot of credit for telling the children to stay calm. Her story also mentioned that Ms. Teacher was proud that when they all saw the huge branch fall right near them, she was sure they understood they needed to get out from under that tree as soon as possible and run to their bus for safety.

Then, Ms. Teacher explained the most important part of this story. She told them, if we didn't have thunder, we wouldn't have any warning. And lightning is very dangerous.

After that, all of the kids understood why their teacher had told them to count while running after a new lightning flash so they wouldn't be distracted by the thunder that followed and could reach safety. She explained further that if we didn't have thunder we might just run under a tree and wait for the rain to stop, but that would be the worst to do. Lightning could hit the tree and the tree could break and fall. Then, Ms. Teacher asked, "What's the best thing to do if you are outdoors and you don't see lightning, but you see dark clouds and you hear thunder?"

Billy stood up from his seat without raising his hand, and yelled, "Run for cover! Run, run, run!" and even though he hadn't raised his hand, all the class laughed including Ms. Teacher.

Then, Suzy shared an important idea, after raising her hand, and said, "If you are indoors when it happens, stay away from the windows?"

Ms. Teacher agreed, "Yes, Suzy. Then, after you are in a safe place, think of happy things to do when it's over. You can also count during a thunderstorm and that's sort of a game but it's an important game and you all counted after you saw the streak of lightning so that you were able count and run to the school bus for shelter. Do you know that counting like that also tells you how near or far away that bolt of lightning is?"

The kids showed a lot of interest then, and nodded agreement.

Suzy, raising her hand, asked, "So, how do you do that again, to check the thunder after lightning?"

Ms. Teacher added, "Just start counting slowly and add the word "and" after each number, like the second hand of a clock that we learned about in class. I'll try to show you but we need to see a lightning bolt."

When Grandma told me this story so I could get over being afraid of thunder, she told me that a huge streak of lightning flashed and everyone in the school bus jumped and screamed. But teacher stayed calm and started to count slowly and the children sat back down and counted along with her. Soon enough, a huge bolt of thunder sounded only after the count of ten. So, the lightning they realized was close by but not as close as before. Then Ms. Teacher taught something new and amazing, "Thunder and lightning occur at the exact same time. It's a "trick of science" because lightning's light travels faster than thunder's sound. If you wait to hear thunder, you may get confused about when to take shelter, but thunder is still a good signal because now we've learned what to do."

At that point, Suzy asked, "So, is a school bus a safe place to be in a thunderstorm?" Her classmates appeared worried after Suzy asked her question and Ms. Teacher responded quickly.

"Yes, Suzy, a school bus is a safe place to take shelter because a car or a bus will carry the electricity through the outside metal of the vehicle so if lightning strikes the lightning is "grounded" by the vehicle. That's an electrical term."

Grandma always laughed whenever she told the next part of the story because Billy jumped up again, without raising his hand, and called out, "Oh, I know about electricity. My Dad says electricity is dangerous and can give you a bad shock and hurt you a lot."

Ms. Teacher was pleased even though Billy had as usual not raised his hand, "Yes, Billy. Lightning is electricity! The electricity in lightning is just as dangerous and can be more dangerous and hurt you worse."

Suzy had drawn a picture by that time and held it up to show her classmates, "Look, I drew a picture of us so scared and lightning hitting that tree. I think it shows what can happen to us if we forget that thunder is a warning and a signal and thunder helps us to stay safe."

Ms. Teacher was pleased, she thanked Suzy, and shared that, "We sure never want what your picture shows to happen to anyone ever! "

I remember Grandma telling me that after that, all the children relaxed and nodded in agreement. Ms. Teacher also made sure to explain that most important of all, thunder is good and when she did that, all of the class understood and happily chimed in to say, "If we didn't have thunder it sure would be hard to stay out of lightning's way!" with lots of laughter and calm reassurance.

Most important of all, the message I learned to overcome my worry about thunder was it doesn't matter who you are or where you live, lightning is dangerous. It can affect and hurt anyone! But, thunder is good because just like the kids in Grandpa's story, as told by Grandma, "If we didn't have thunder it sure would be hard to stay out of lightning's way!"

Grandma also told me that after that day, Suzy, realized something important about Billy, and Suzy told him, "Thank you Billy, for helping, I guess you are not a bragger after all; you just want to share things that you know."

Ms. Teacher was also happy and suggested they all sing a song and have some fun since the bus driver had started driving the school bus back to the school where the children's parents would meet them.

Turns out the children made up two songs. They liked each song and sang them on the way back. The songs were:

SONG:

It's raining,

It's pouring.

The thunder is roaring.

I'll count in my head.

I'm sheltered instead.

It's gonna be over by morning.

SONG:

It's raining. It's pouring.

I've got thunder's sound in my head.

But I don't care. The lightning's out there.

So, I'll stay in a safe place instead.

I still remember each song from when I solved my worry about being afraid of thunder with Grandma Annie's help and storytelling. I'm sure Grandma's re-telling it sent an important message to Jimmy, and Theodore, too.

It sure had been an awesome, eventful and surprising day but also a day to learn something very new and important in order to get over being afraid of thunder. All the children felt real lucky and very confident about learning how to solve a real worry.

CHAPTER 5
A New Afraid of Thunder Worry

heard later what happened after Grandma Annie finished telling Jimmy (and Theodore) the story that Grandpa had told to her. I wanted to know if it had helped Jimmy to get over being worried about thunder happening again and making him afraid.

Grandma told me, she asked Jimmy, "Now that you've heard this story, I hope you've learned one of the most important things you'll ever need to know about not being afraid of thunder."

Jimmy was absolutely convinced and told her that he agreed that if we didn't have thunder it sure would be hard to get to a safe place as quickly as possible.

Grandma was glad that Jimmy agreed. But then Grandma found out there was another worry that the thunder had caused. Jimmy explained to Grandma that when a noisy loud noise happened suddenly especially like thunder it made him put his hands over his ears to make the sound go away and stop.

Jimmy commented, "That's the same thing the children did in the story you told us ...oops I mean me (he looked sheepishly at Theodore) about Grandpa when he was a boy."

Grandma thought for a moment, and said, "Oh, I see. So, you were afraid of thunder, but you got over it, except now, you have another worry."

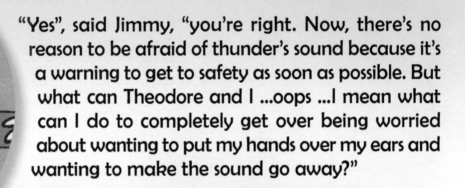

"Yes", said Jimmy, "you're right. Now, there's no reason to be afraid of thunder's sound because it's a warning to get to safety as soon as possible. But what can Theodore and I ...oops ...I mean what can I do to completely get over being worried about wanting to put my hands over my ears and wanting to make the sound go away?"

"Hmmmm," Grandma mused, "I think I know something that will help. It's something you can do instead of putting your hands over your ears whenever these types of noises happen, even though those sounds are helping. They are of course warnings that danger can be near and as quickly as possible to get out of the way. So would you like to know what to do if the sound of thunder is very bothersome?"

Yes," replied Jimmy laughing, "I don't like going around with my hands over my ears. I might miss out when it's time for dinner, or we're going to watch a video. Or, that there's no more thunder! I sure would look silly to Theodore....I mean to everyone."

Then, everyone, even Theodore I'm sure, had a huge laugh. Once everyone got back to normal, Grandma explained further, "The loud sound that thunder makes is a warning that danger is near, and we need to stay out of the way of any lightning. So, here is something I mentioned earlier to help."

Grandma Annie moved next to Jimmy. She picked up Jimmy's toy xylophone, and placed it on her lap. Then she picked up the xylophone mallet hammer and hit the largest key on the xylophone to produce a loud, low sound.

Jimmy jumped up from his bed covers and was quick to say, "Sorry, Grandma that doesn't sound much like thunder."

Grandma agreed. "I know. How about if I just knock my fist on this table?"

Jimmy nodded, "That'll work, but Mom or Dad might not like hearing it."

"Hah, ha," laughed Grandma and she vaguely thought she noticed a glimmer of humor from Theodore too. "Okay, I agree. So, let me do this again" and she struck the xylophone key like before. "There, did you hear that?"

"Yes, and I bet you're going to tell me that I just need to use my imagination to make that sound like a loud crashing thunderbolt."

"Well, Jimmy, we don't have much choice, and do you remember that using your imagination helps exercise your brain just like riding a bicycle helps exercise your arms and legs?"

Grandma never mentioned Jimmy's and most likely Theodore's reaction but I'm sure they were both "all ears".

Grandma continued, "So, now I need you to think of the light that lightning makes and begin counting like Ms. Teacher taught her class in my story."

Grandma started counting with Jimmy and she almost thought she caught an action to show that Theodore was also doing some type of counting. Anyway, after the count of 3, Grandma slammed the mallet against the largest key to sound like thunder and to show lightning was about 3 miles away.

"We'll try again, and when I ping the mallet on the littlest key, use your imagination and pretend that lightning is striking. When I smack the mallet on the largest key, that will be for the sound of thunder. When that happens, the last number you counted will be just about how many miles away the lightning was and because you were using your imagination and focusing on counting, you completely forgot about putting your hands over your ears, right?"

"Gotit, Grandma! Wow, that's neat", Jimmy smiled and gave a thumb's up to Theodore and to Grandma.

Grandma smiled, "Yes, I know, but no talking now. Just listen for the imaginary lightning, then begin counting in your mind until you hear the mallet hit for the imaginary thunder. Let's try it again. I will count out loud just to help. "

"Can you knock on the table just one time to make it awesome?" To the best of my knowledge and knowing how Grandma always worked to help her grandchildren, I am sure that by then Jimmy and most likely Theodore were in bed with covers drawn close under the chin and ready to count without speaking.

"Okay, Jimmy. Here we go, again."

I am totally sure that Grandma must have knocked on the table and Jimmy had counted in his head nodding as he counted each number thinking one.... and.... two.... and...three... and...four...and five because then something interesting happened.

Jimmy was starting to yawn and could hardly keep his eyes open. He yawned again and then said, yawning, "I could imagine the lightning flashed and I was counting in my mind and when you slammed with the mallet I could even imagine a great clap of thunder in the sky."

Grandma Annie was super happy to hear that, and said, "This time the sound will be softer. We can pretend the thunder isn't as loud as before and that it's going farther and farther away and that will mean you will need to count more numbers...are you okay with that?"

Jimmy yawned from his bed, and said, "I'm sure I can count a lot more numbers and use my imagination the way you said."

Grandma agreed, "Good, so here we go." She "pinged" the mallet softly and then started to count softly saying, "One.... and... two... and three... and four... and five... and six... and seven.... and eight...." She counted up to ten and then pinged the largest key very, very softly. "Well, that would have been about 10 miles away," she marveled, then exclaimed, " oh ...my goodness, look at you, Jimmy."

To the best of Grandma Annie's recollection, Jimmy must have been counting... and then stopped... completely drifting off to dreamland.

CHAPTER SIX
All Thunder Worries Solved

Grandma mused, "Oh, he's gone to sleep just like before when he was afraid of the dark and I helped him get over it with another story. I guess using his imagination for counting helped him fall asleep or maybe he just had a long day. I know that when he wakes, he won't ever be afraid of thunder again. I'll be able to congratulate him too."

Grandma gave it some more thought, "I'm sorry I also didn't have time to mention many other noises and sounds that help us. Like the loud sound of a tea kettle whistle. Also, the alarm clock sound to get out of bed and start the day. Even the noisy annoying sounds that big trucks and trash vehicles make when backing up because of potential danger. Or a big tractor trailer backing up and persons jumping out of the way. When sounds are loud and annoying, they still help us know that we need to take action to stay alert and not put our hands over our ears."

Later, the next time I saw Grandma she was very excited to give me the recorder with all the story material she had completed. "It was so fun, "she explained, "The only thing is that I'm not sure I included everything that I wanted to. Also, I didn't remind Jimmy that thunder is also a challenge! It's loud and even scary; but you can meet that challenge by choosing to stay focused and counting while using your imagination, like we did."

I agreed, and told Grandma, "That's what you taught me so long ago."

Grandma smiled at me then, and softly said, "I should tell you after that day, in the story Grandpa told me, if anyone asked him, "Are you afraid of thunder?" he'd make a whistling sound ...then say, thunder is a signal.

If we didn't have thunder, it sure would be hard to stay out of the way of lightning."

Then, Grandma gave it even more thought, and said, "Maybe I won't need to tell Jimmy after all because he got over it."

As an added note, because Grandma has such an interest in using our imagination, I'm sure I know exactly what happened after Jimmy fell asleep.

Grandma Annie started to rock slowly in her rocker, and softly, just above a whisper, said, "I love you, Jimmy". Also, if I'm not mistaken, she never questioned whether Theodore wondered if she loved him, and she simply said, "I love you too, Theodore."

I didn't have to be there, right then, to know Grandma was sitting back smiling, closing her eyes, rocking and waiting for the next worry to solve. She's very wise, and we all love her very much.

The End.

As the author, I have made every effort to ensure the information in this book at press time was accurate and correct. However, I urge you to find out more about Lightning and Thunder Facts and Myths by visiting https://www.noaa.gov the official national weather service website.

Stay safe!